D0961544

PLANTS VS. ZOMBIES™

GARDEN WARFARE

Written by **PAUL TOBIN**

Art by **TIM LATTIE**

Colors by **MATT J. RAINWATER**

Letters by **STEVE DUTRO**

Cover by **TIM LATTIE**

DARK HORSE BOOKS

PLANTS VS. ZOMBIES
GARDEN WARFARE

Publisher **MIKE RICHARDSON**
Senior Editor **PHILIP R. SIMON**
Associate Editor **MEGAN WALKER**
Designer **BRENNAN THOME**
Digital Art Technician **CHRISTINA McKENZIE**

Special thanks to everyone at Electronic Arts and PopCap Games, especially Alexandria Land, A.J. Rathbun, Kristen Star, Amanda Doiron, Kevin Lee, Justin Wiebe, Emerson Oaks, and Kyle Duncan.

First Edition: September 2018
ISBN 978-1-50670-548-4

1 2 3 4 5 6 7 8 9 10
Printed in China

DarkHorse.com | PopCap.com

No plants were harmed in the making of this graphic novel. However, the Cookie Store did receive a lot of angry fan mail for not actually selling any cookies, mostly from the hungry people who worked on this book; the editors did get their toes run over by Scooter's scooter during a wild game of freeze tag; and Deadbeard underwent a painful, month-long process of getting all of those stickers off of him.

PLANTS vs. ZOMBIES: GARDEN WARFARE VOLUME 2 | Published by Dark Horse Books, a division of Dark Horse Comics, Inc., 10956 SE Main Street, Milwaukie, OR 97222 | To find a comics shop in your area, visit comicshoplocator.com |

Library of Congress Cataloging-in-Publication Data

Names: Tobin, Paul, 1965- author. | Lattie, Tim, artist. | Rainwater, Matthew J., colourist. | Dutro, Steve, letterer.
Title: Plants vs. zombies. Garden warfare volume 2 / written by Paul Tobin ; art by Tim Lattie ; colors by Matt J. Rainwater ; letters by Steve Dutro.
Other titles: Plants versus zombies. Garden warfare | Garden warfare volume 2
Description: First edition. | Milwaukie, OR : Dark Horse Books, September 2018. | Based on the video game Plants vs. Zombies. | Summary: "Zombies have taken over and forced neighborhood defenders Nate, Patrice, and their fearless plants back on their heels! Not all hope is lost however when an unlikely plant hero comes to the rescue with the fate of Neighborville at stake!"-- Provided by publisher.
Identifiers: LCCN 2018015854 | ISBN 9781506705484 (hardback)
Subjects: LCSH: Graphic novels. | CYAC: Graphic novels. | Science fiction. | Plants--Fiction. | Zombies--Fiction. | BISAC: JUVENILE FICTION / Comics & Graphic Novels / Media Tie-In. | JUVENILE FICTION / Comics & Graphic Novels / General.
Classification: LCC PZ7.7.T62 Pic 2018 | DDC 741.5/973--dc23
LC record available at https://lccn.loc.gov/2018015854

DEAR DIARY...ME AND BELCHER VON BOOMTHROAT JUST GOT BACK TO TOWN, AND IT SEEMS **STRANGE.** WHERE **IS** EVERYONE?
BELCH!

THERE ARE LOTS OF DOGS AND CATS COWERING BENEATH TRASH CANS.

AND PEOPLE WHISPERING TO ME FROM BOARDED-UP STORES.
BEE WEAR
BEWARE! BEWARE! BEWARE!

BELCHER DID ONE OF HIS SOFTEST BELCHES, BUT EVEN THAT SCARED ALL THE DOGS AND CATS AWAY.
BELCH!
MEOWRR
bark!
bark!
RRRUFF!
hssst!

SO, IT MAKES ME WONDER WHAT'S BEEN HAPPENING IN NEIGHBORVILLE SINCE--

HEY!
GRAB!

gulp!
GULP!
OKAY, STILL NOT SURE WHAT'S HAPPENING HERE IN NEIGHBORVILLE, BUT ONE THING I *AM* SURE ABOUT IS THAT IT'S--
TIME TO RUN!
AHH! *MORE* ZOMBIES!
AND EVEN *MORE!*
PLUS, SOME *ADDITIONAL* ONES!
TIME OUT!

WHEW. *THANKS.*
SORRY ABOUT THIS. *HUFF HUFF* BUT IT'S THESE *BOOTS!*

SORRY TO HAVE TO MAKE YOU WAIT, BUT IT'S *SO* HARD TO RUN IN HIKING BOOTS.
NEW FRANTIC FLEA!
GIVE ME A SECOND TO CHANGE INTO SOME *SHOES*, WILL YOU?

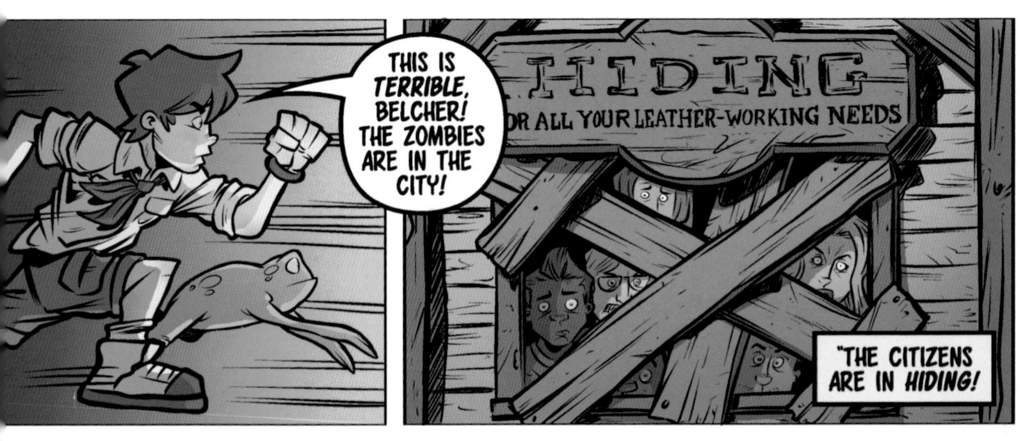
THIS IS TERRIBLE, BELCHER! THE ZOMBIES ARE IN THE CITY!
HIDING
FOR ALL YOUR LEATHER-WORKING NEEDS
"THE CITIZENS ARE IN HIDING!

"RADIO STATIONS ARE PLAYING ZOMBOSS' TERRIBLE POP MUSIC!"
I EAT BRAINS,
BELCH!
AND I DON'T FLOSS.
I RULE THIS CITY!
AND MY NAME'S ZOMBOSS!

"THERE'S A ZOMBIE!

"THERE'S A ZOMBIE!

BRAINS?
BRAINS?
BRAINS?
"THERE'S MORE ZOMBIES!

"THERE'S A DUCK WHO STOLE MY HIKING BOOTS!"

WHOA!
STOP
STOP!

IS THAT SUPER BRAINZ?
HE'S HERE, TOO? WHAT'S GOING ON?!

"YOU GOT A PROBLEM?"
MOVE-IT!?
HMM? TRUCK BLOCKS STREET!

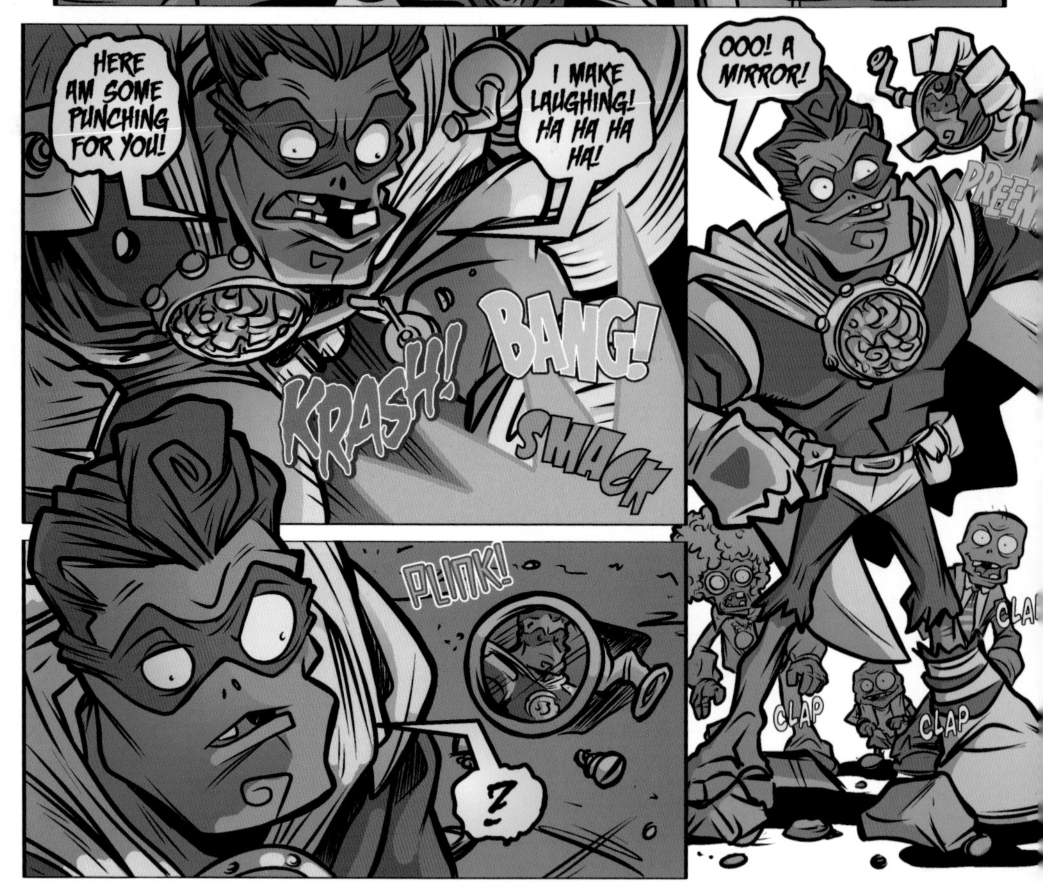
HERE AM SOME PUNCHING FOR YOU!
I MAKE LAUGHING! HA HA HA HA!
KRASH!
BANG!
SMACK
PLINK!
?
OOO! A MIRROR!
CLAP
CLAP

BELCH?
GOOD QUESTION, BELCHER.
I ONLY WISH I COULD ANSWER THAT.
BELCH!

"SEVEN DAYS AGO, YOU AND I STARTED OUR CAMPING TRIP, SEARCHING GLITTERBALL FOREST FOR...

"...THE LEGENDARY DISCO CHOMPER!
"CRAZY DAVE WANTED US TO FIND HIM, BEFRIEND HIM, GIVE HIM A NAME...

"...AND DEFINITELY ASK HIM FOR FASHION ADVICE."
BLOGGON PLANG BOOGIE MOOG OOGIE!

"UNFORTUN-ATELY, WE COULDN'T FIND HIM, AND ALSO I RAN OUT OF MY FAVORITE SNACK, PEANUT BUTTER PIZZA SQUARES."
OH, NO! THE LAST ONE?
BELCH!

BUT WE'VE ONLY BEEN GONE A WEEK.
AND WE'VE COME BACK TO... THIS.

"THE ARCHITECTURE HAS GONE...WEIRD."

I'M PRETTY SURE I DON'T REMEMBER THAT STATUE.

AND...
WHOOOSH!!!

...I DON'T REMEMBER MR. STUBBINS HAVING THIS HAMSTER TRAIL HIGHWAY.
SQUICK!

I WONDER WHAT HAPPENED?
ZOMBIES TAKE OVER CITY
BVIOUSLY!
BELCH!

OH, NO! THAT WAS YOUR WARNING BELCH!
BUT...WHAT'S WRONG, BELCHER?
IF ONLY YOU COULD TALK!
IF ONLY YOU COULD GIVE ME SOME HINT, NO MATTER HOW SMALL, AS TO WHAT YOU'RE TRYING TO WARN ME ABOUT!
BELCH! BELCH!
WAVE WAVE
OH.
ZOMBIES. GOT IT.
GET IT YET?
BUT THEY WON'T GET US!
I'LL USE THIS MANHOLE COVER AS A SHIELD!
GRRRR!
STRAIN!
URFFF!
STRAIN!
HRGGGHH!
STRAIN!

FOR NO PARTICULAR REASON, I CHANGED MY MIND! LET'S *RUN*, BELCHER!

OH, NO! THE WAY IS *BLOCKED!*
WE'LL HAVE TO GO *THIS* WAY AND...

STO
OH, NO! BLOCKED AGAIN!

NO PASSING ZONE
AND *ALSO* BLOCKED!

THE PLANTS HAVE SPROUTED,
AND MUSHROOMED!
BUT THE HUMANS KNOW,
THEY'RE STILL QUITE DOOMED!
UGH! THAT HORRIBLE MUSIC!

THE END
For all your end table needs
LOOKS LIKE THIS IS...*THE END.*

PAPFF!
BAFF!
THWOPP!
BWONKK!
BRAINS?
WHAT WAS THAT?
WHOOSH!!
WELCOME TO Pop's
POP!
POP!
POP!
THUMP!
THUMP!
BOING!
SCREECH

SCOOTER!

Date Boards
KER-SPLANG!
FWAPP!
P-BLAMM!

BOFF!
BRAINS?
THWOPP
!!
??
SPAFF!
FOPP!

BRAINS?
THWOOSH!
!!
ROLL!
??
ROLL!
ZOOOM

HOORAY!
WE'RE SAVED!

UH-OH.

Gumball Grab!

PAFF!
PAFF!
PAFF!
Gumball Attack!

Gumball Maelstrom!
PAFF!
PAFF!
PAFF!
PAFF!
PAFF!

Chocolate Flavored Gumball!
AH, THIS ONE'S TOO DELICIOUS TO THROW!
CHEW CHEW CHOMP

GRAB!

Gumball Attack!
THWAK!
AHH! YOUR GUMBALL ATTACK IS ADMITTEDLY BETTER THAN MINE!

NOT GOOD!
WE CAN'T HOLD THEM OFF, UNLESS...
BELCH!

HOCKEY STICKS!

SNAP! SNAP!
SHATTER

OOO! PIZZA FLAVORED GUMBALL!

BRAAAINS...

BELCH!
BELCH!

OOO! YOUR FEAR BELCH!

BELCH!
AH! MY FEAR BELCH!

NATE!
BELCH!
OOPS! MY SURPRISE BELCH!

OOO?
AN ANGEL?

HUH?
NO, IT'S ME.

Patrice Blazing!

FIRE!!!!

HUH? FIRE?
WHERE?

OH. SORRY. NO. I WAS TALKING TO MY PLANTS, TELLING THEM TO OPEN FIRE.
YOU CAN RUN AWAY NOW.
CONSIDER IT DONE!

OPEN FIRE!!!
P-TOO
THOOK
P-BLAMM!
P-BLAMM!
P-TOO
THOOK
THAPP
SPLUTT
THAPP
SPLUTT

WE DID IT! THEY'RE RUNNING AWAY!
High Five!
SPROINGG!

YEAH! AND WE'RE RUNNING AWAY, TOO! WE'VE GOT TO GET TO SAFETY BEFORE THEY SEND FOR REIN-FORCEMENTS!
HURRY!
BELCH!
WE ARE HURRYING! THAT'S HIS HURRYING BELCH!

AND SOON...
OKAY. WE'RE SAFE HERE. OR, AS SAFE AS IT GETS.
BUT I DON'T UNDERSTAND WHAT HAPPENED? HOW DID THE ZOMBIES TAKE OVER NEIGHBORVILLE IN THE SHORT TIME I WAS GONE?
FROPPALULU BIFFLE PLINKTON!
JUST WHAT MY UNCLE DAVE SAYS.
IT WAS ZOMBOSS, OF COURSE.
"YOU REMEMBER THAT ROBOTIC BUTT HE HAD FROM THE FUTURE? WE MANAGED TO WRECK IT, BUT IT TURNS OUT THE BUTT WAS POWERED BY A FUTURE GAS.
AMERICAN ZOMBIE WARRIOR
"AND THEN SOME OF THAT HELIUM-LIKE GAS ESCAPED FROM THE BROKEN BUTT..."
EH?
PFFFT!
"ZOMBOSS WAS ABLE TO CAPTURE THAT GAS AND--WORKING WITH HIS SCIENTISTS--USED IT TO FILL HIS BALLOONS, MAKING THE BALLOON ZOMBIES LIGHTNING QUICK!
"THEY WERE SUDDENLY ZOOMING EVERYWHERE AT UNBELIEVABLE SPEEDS! ATTACKING BEFORE WE KNEW THEY WERE THERE! LEAVING BEFORE WE COULD REACT!
"AND WHEN WE WERE REELING, ZOMBOSS' GROUND FORCES MARCHED IN.
"ONE BY ONE, OUR DEFENSES FELL. WE COULDN'T STOP THEM!

"LUCKILY, THE BUTT SOON RAN OUT OF GAS."
SPUTTER
CURSES! AND YET, IT'S FAR TOO LATE FOR CRAZY DAVE AND THOSE CHILDREN TO STOP ME NOW!
"ZOMBOSS MAY BE RIGHT. NEIGHBORVILLE IS OVERRUN WITH ZOMBIES NOW, AND WE CAN'T SEEM TO WIN BACK ANY OF THE TERRITORY.

"EVERYONE IS IN HIDING. OLD MAN CORRIGAN IS RUNNING HIS ICE CREAM SHOP FROM BENEATH THE STREETS.
ICE CREAM! (KNOCK FOUR TIMES)

"YOUNG MAN CORRIGAN IS OPERATING HIS CAT-SITTING BUSINESS FROM THE OLD OAK TREE IN TOWN SQUARE.

"EVERYWHERE YOU GO, YOU HAVE TO KNOCK FOUR TIMES ON A DOOR IN ORDER TO PROVE YOU'RE HUMAN..."

KNOCK! KNOCK!
KNOCK! KNOCK!
"...SINCE ZOMBIES CAN'T COUNT PAST THREE."

ELSEWHERE...
IMPORTANT ZOMBIE PSYCHIATRIST OFFICE
THANK YOU FOR SEEING ME TODAY.
I JUST FELT THE NEED TO TALK.
TO EXPRESS WHAT I'M FEELING IN THIS, THE TIME OF MY TRIUMPH!
SO MANY PEOPLE THINK THAT I'M UNFEELING. IT'S NOT TRUE. I HAVE MANY FEELINGS.
CLAP CLAP CLAP
PRIDE, FOR ONE. AND CRUELTY, OF COURSE. SUPERIORITY. AND SELF-IMPORTANCE!
I ALSO HAVE SOME BAD FEELINGS, TOO.
THE POINT IS, EVEN I'M OVERWHELMED BY JOY AT TIMES, SUCH AS NOW, SINCE MY ZOMBIE ARMY HAS MANAGED TO TAKE OVER THE CITY...
...PLUNGING NEIGHBORVILLE'S CITIZENS INTO HORROR AND SYSTEMATICALLY DESTROYING THE HARMONY THEY'VE CREATED.
WHO WOULDN'T BE PROUD OF SUCH AN ACCOMPLISHMENT?
AND SO, I WANTED TO SHARE MY FEELINGS OF JOY WITH THE WISEST, SMARTEST, MOST INCISIVE PERSON I'VE EVER KNOWN.
YOU.

SO WHAT I'M TRYING TO TELL YOU, NATE, IS THAT THINGS ARE HORRIBLE RIGHT NOW.

EVERYTHING IS SO BEAUTIFUL RIGHT NOW!

PEOPLE CAN'T GO ANYWHERE WITHOUT BEING IN TERROR.

PEOPLE CAN'T GO ANYWHERE WITHOUT BEING IN TERROR!

LUCKILY, WE'RE BUILDING A RESISTANCE ARMY.
WAVE WAVE
WAVE WAVE

THERE WILL BE NO RESISTANCE!

NOBODY KNOWS WHAT TO DO. NEIGHBORVILLE IS FILLED WITH *CONFUSION*.

WHY IS THAT DUCK IN BOOTS?
THUMP THUMP
WADDLE WADDLE

RATTLE
RATTLE
RATTLE
OH, NO! THE TIN CANS!

RATTLE
RATTLE
WHAT'S WRONG? WHAT'S WITH THE TIN CANS?
IT'S A WARNING SYSTEM! WHENEVER THE ZOMBIES ARE TRYING TO BREAK IN SOME-WHERE...
"...NEIGHBORVILLE'S CITIZENS CAN TUG ON ONE OF THE STRINGS WE'VE SET UP..."
TUG!
TUG!!
TUG!!!
RATTLE
RATTLE
RATTLE
...AND IT RATTLES A CAN TO LET US KNOW THEY NEED HELP!
DUCK DUCK GOOSE PARK
HICKORY DICKORY CLOCKS
HUBBARDS CUBBOARDS
WAIT, DOES THAT MEAN THERE'S AN ATTACK AT THE COOKIE STORE?!?!
RATTLE
The Cookie Store
RATTLE
YES. THAT'S RIGHT. WE SHOULD--
PREPARE FOR BATTLE!
ON THIS DAY, WE FIGHT FOR COOKIES!

BRING THAT NEW FRIEND OF YOURS!
YOU MEAN SCOOTER?
THAT'S HIS NAME?
HELLO, SCOOTER!
WE NEED TO FIGHT ZOMBIES. ARE YOU WILLING TO HELP?
SCOOT!!!
I THINK THAT MEANS "YES"!
IT ALSO MEANS... LET'S GET GOING!
SAVE THE COOKIE STORE!

OON...
THERE IT IS! GET READY, EVERYONE!
The Cookie Store
All kinds

FIRE!
P-TOO
P-TOO
THWOOP
THWOOP
P-TOO

"IT'S NO GOOD! THEIR ARMOR IS TOO STRONG!"
THAPP THAPP
THAPP THAPP
B-TINGG! B-TONGG!

FRED'S
FISHING POLES
mike's
magnets
I JUST MIGHT HAVE AN IDEA.
YOU MEAN... ATTACH MAGNETS TO FISHING POLES AND USE THEM TO PLUCK THE ARMOR OFF THE ZOMBIES?

Candy
-time-
"is it really time ?"
UH, NO.
I MEANT WE SHOULD GO TO THE CANDY STORE AND STOCK UP ON SNACKS...
...BUT YOUR IDEA IS PROBABLY BETTER.

OON...
B-TINGG!
THAPP!
THWOOSH
THWOOP
BRAINS?

OKAY! THE ARMOR IS GONE, AND THE GAME IS ON!
LET 'EM HAVE IT, GUYS!
SELFIE!
SCOOTER AND THE OTHERS HAVE DRIVEN OFF ALL THE ZOMBIES EXCEPT THAT MASSIVE GARGANTUAR. ANY IDEAS?
HMM. I'M THINKING. I'M... THINKING.
ARE YOU THINKING ABOUT TRICKING HIM INTO THIS PIT, OR IS IT THAT CANDY THING AGAIN?
PETE'S PITS
ALL OUR PITS GUARANTEED BOTTOMLESS!
UH, IT'S THE CANDY THING AGAIN.
DISPLAY PIT
"CAUTION! BE ADVISED, I GUESS."
OON.
GRRAWRR-BEAR! PUNCH HIS TOES!
BELCH!
THONKK!
ARRRR!

NOW, NATE! DROP THE MAGNET IN!
FLOOP
AND THEN...
THWOOSH
SMACK
WHACK
THANNG
PERFECT! HE'S ATTRACTING THE HELMETS! NOW, IF I'VE PLANNED THIS RIGHT...
"...HE SHOULD BLINDLY WALK INTO THE DISPLAY PIT AT PETE'S PITS!"
STUMBLE
TOPPLE!!
PETE'S PITS "WE'RE THE PITS"
HA! PERFECT. HE'LL NEVER GET OUT OF THERE!
YOU KNOW, THEY REALLY SHOULDN'T LEAVE THEIR PITS OUTSIDE LIKE THIS.
The Cookie Store All kinds
of things EXCEPT cookies!
BUT, WHATEVER. AT LEAST WE SAVED THE COOKIE STORE. LET'S HAVE SOME COOKIES!
UH, THEY DON'T HAVE COOKIES, NATE.
NOOOOOOOO!

OON.
WELL, EVEN IF I DON'T HAVE ANY COOKIES, AT LEAST I KNOW WHAT'S GOING ON, NOW.
THE ZOMBIES...

...HAVE TAKEN OVER ALMOST THE ENTIRE CITY, MAKING THINGS...

...TERRIBLE! BUT AT LEAST THE CITIZENS ARE SAFE INSIDE THEIR HOMES. ZOMBOSS HASN'T MANAGED TO...

...EAT A SINGLE BRAIN! SO FRUST-RATING! AND THOSE REMAINING POCKETS OF RESISTANCE! ALL THOSE PLANTS! CRAZY DAVE AND THOSE CHILDREN! THEY STOP ME AT EVERY TURN!
SO, THE QUESTION IS...

...WHAT ARE WE GOING TO DO ABOUT ALL THIS?

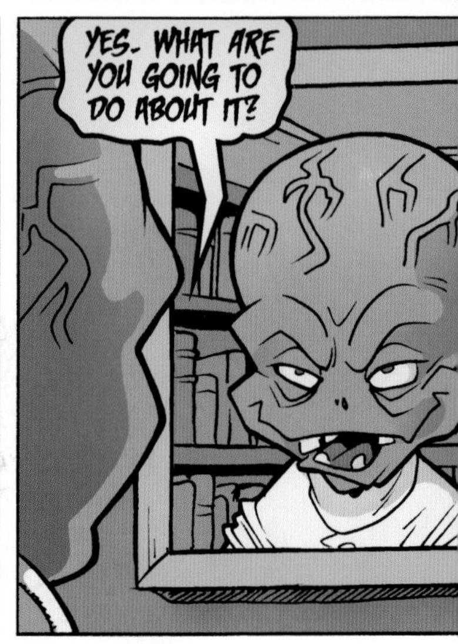
YES. WHAT ARE YOU GOING TO DO ABOUT IT?

OTHER QUESTIONS TO CONSIDER!
HEY, IF NEIGHBORVILLE'S STORES ARE ALL CLOSED, WHERE CAN I BUY MORE PEANUT BUTTER PIZZA SNACKS?

HMM, IS THE SECOND SEASON OF PACHYDERM P.I. STREAMING YET?

ARE YOU EVER GOING TO WASH YOUR CAMPING CLOTHES?
SNIFF SNIFF

!
MR. STUBBINS? DID YOU TAKE THE BATTERIES FROM MY EGO POLISHER?

BRAPP-BOODLE CRANN-GROTTLETONGUE?!

YOU HAVE ANY IDEA WHAT HE JUST SAID?
NOPE. THAT'S ANOTHER QUESTION.

BUT I SUPPOSE THE MAIN QUESTION IS: "HOW ARE WE GOING TO STOP ZOMBOSS?"

PLUS, THAT THING ABOUT WASHING YOUR CLOTHES.
SNIFF SNIFF

AT LEAST THERE'S NO QUESTION WHAT MY NEXT STEP WILL BE, MR. STUBBINS.
FIZZLE
"AFTER MY OLD PLAN WITH THIS METALLIC BUTT RAN OUT OF GAS..."
...I'VE REALIZED SOMETHING THAT I SHOULD HAVE ADMITTED LONG AGO.

I'M NO GOOD AT PLAYING FAIR.
GRAB!
GRAB!
GRAB!

#1 CHEAT
UNFAIR
LUCKILY, I'M NATURALLY AND SUPREMELY TALENTED AT PLAYING UNFAIR.
DECEIVER OF THE YEAR
ARTIST

AND I'VE COME TO UNDERSTAND THAT WHAT'S ALLOWING THE YUMMY CITIZENS OF NEIGHBORVILLE TO REMAIN IN HIDING IS...POWER!

"THE POWER TO RUN THEIR AIR-CONDITIONERS AND THEIR STOVES AND THEIR LIGHTS AND..."

NO ZOMBIES PLEASE!
...THEIR ANNOYINGLY BRIGHT "NO ZOMBIES, PLEASE!" NEON DOOR SIGNS.
SO, I HAVE TO STOP THIS POWER.
AND SINCE THIS ENTIRE TOWN IS RUN ON SOLAR ENERGY...

...I JUST HAVE TO COVER THE SOLAR PANELS, AND THEY'LL SOON LOSE ALL POWER! HA HA HA HA HA HA!
SOLAR PANELS!

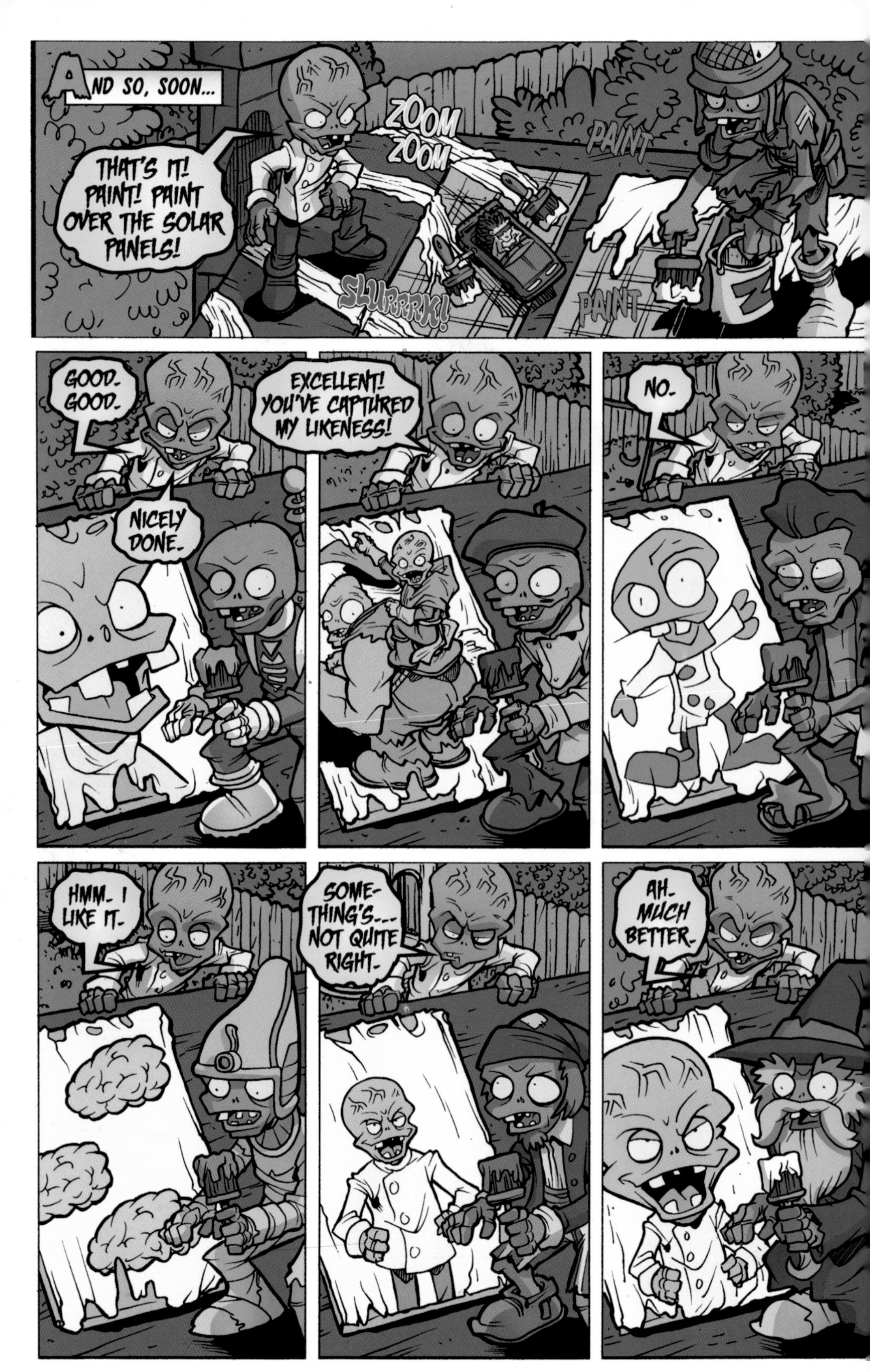
AND SO, SOON...
THAT'S IT! PAINT! PAINT OVER THE SOLAR PANELS!
ZOOM ZOOM
PAINT
SLURRRK!
PAINT
GOOD. GOOD.
NICELY DONE.
EXCELLENT! YOU'VE CAPTURED MY LIKENESS!
NO.
HMM. I LIKE IT.
SOME-THING'S... NOT QUITE RIGHT.
AH. MUCH BETTER.

AND THEN, NOT LONG AFTER...
WE HAVE TO GET THAT PAINT OFF THE SOLAR PANELS!

BUT...
THIS PAINT IS WICKED STRONG, AND TOTALLY PERMANENT! WHAT THE HECK IS IT MADE OF?
UGH! IT'S NOT COMING OFF!

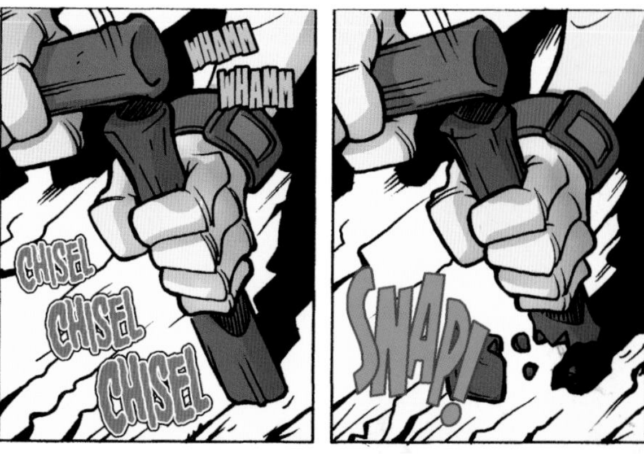
WHAMM
WHAMM
CHISEL
CHISEL
CHISEL
SNAP!

SO, UNFORTUNATELY...
GAHH! WE DIDN'T MANAGE TO CLEAR AWAY A SINGLE CHIP OF PAINT!
THIS IS TERRIBLE! THE CITY WILL LOSE POWER!
PLUS, WE HAVE TO KEEP LOOKING AT ALL THESE ZOMBOSS PORTRAITS.

N NOT LONG...
KRRITCH
HONEY! IS THE WATER HEATER WORKING?

BOBO FLINGLE?
CLICK
CLICK
CLICK

OH, NO! OUR KITTY CAT CONVEYOR BELT ISN'T WORKING!
MWRR?
THE CATS ARE STRANDED!

THIS IS HORRIBLE, NATE! BECAUSE OF ZOMBOSS' TERRIBLE PAINT, AND THOSE EQUALLY TERRIBLE PAINTINGS, NEIGHBORVILLE IS WITHERING!
WE NEED TO DO SOMETHING! WE HAVE TO STOP ZOMBOSS!
IT'S TIME TO...FIGHT BACK!
YOU'RE RIGHT, PATRICE! IT'S TIME FOR THE REAL BATTLE TO BEGIN... IN EARNEST!

ROBOTS
EARNEST
COOKIES
FOREST
PIRATES
WELL, NOT IN EARNEST, SINCE THAT'S A SUBURB OF NEIGHBORVILLE, BUT YOU GET THE IDEA.

SCOOTER, IF WE'RE GOING TO HAVE *ANY* HOPE OF BEATING ZOMBOSS, WE'RE GOING TO NEED *EVERYONE'S* HELP.
ARE YOU WILLING TO PITCH IN?
BROBBLE FLOBBLE GOBBLE.
UNCLE DAVE SAYS HE'S BEEN TALKING WITH SCOOTER.
"APPARENTLY, SCOOTER WAS RAISED ALONE, AFTER HIS FLOWERPOT FLOATED AWAY FROM HOME ONE TIME WHEN THE ZOMBIES FLOODED NEIGHBORVILLE."
!!!
"SINCE THEN, HE'S SPENT HIS TIME RIDING AROUND ON HIS KICK-SCOOTER, HELPING OUT UNCLE DAVE AND ALSO OTHER PLANTS...
"...DOING ODD JOBS LIKE WASHING WINDOWS, DELIVERING PLANT FOOD, OR SHINING WATERING CANS."
MY UNCLE THINKS THAT BECAUSE OF SCOOTER'S LIFE ON THE STREET, HE MIGHT BE A BIT TOUGHER THAN SOME OF THE OTHER PEASHOOTERS.
PHOOT!
WHAPP!
B-TANG
THWAK!
SMACK
AND HE'S *WICKED* ACCURATE, TOO.

"SCOOTER HAD ADJUSTED TO LIVING ALONE, BUT THEN CAME THE SCIENTIST ZOMBIES WITH THEIR BUTT GAS BALLOONS! SUDDENLY, THERE WAS ILL-SMELLING DANGER EVERYWHERE!

"THEN, AFTER A TERRIBLE WEEK OF FIGHTING ZOMBIES...AND WATCHING ZOMBOSS EATING POP SMARTS, WHICH WAS *TOTALLY* GROSS...

"...SCOOTER MET NATE AND BELCHER VON BOOMTHROAT..."
BELCH!
Level 5 belch!
AWW, LEVEL 10?! YOU WIN AGAIN!
Level 10 belch!
BELCH!

"...AND SCOOTER MET ALL THE *OTHER* PEASHOOTERS...

"...AND SAW THE VALUE OF WORKING AS A TEAM."
P-TOO
P-BLAMM
P-BLAMM
P-TOO
P-BLAMM

"UNFORTUNATELY, ACCORDING TO MY UNCLE DAVE, SCOOTER STILL FEELS LIKE AN OUTCAST, SINCE HE DOESN'T KNOW HOW TO REALLY FIT IN OR UNDER-STAND THE GAMES THE OTHER PEASHOOTERS PLAY."
KICK!
!
ROLL!
BUMP
?
P-BLAMM
P-BLAMM
P-BLAMM
P-BLAMM
THWAKK
BAPP!
WHACK
WHACK
THWAKK
DON'T WORRY ABOUT A FEW GOOF-UPS, SCOOTER. AFTER ALL, EVERYONE LIKES *NATE*, AND *HE* MAKES GIANT MISTAKES ALL THE TIME!
RIGHT! WAIT. WHAT?

SOON...
WITH NEIGHBORVILLE LOSING POWER EVERYWHERE, WE NEED TO PRIORITIZE.

SO I'VE MADE THESE STICKERS, NUMBERED ONE THROUGH ONE HUNDRED, SO WE CAN KEEP TRACK OF WHAT'S MOST IMPORTANT...
#1
...LIKE THE FIRE DEPARTMENT, AND THE POLICE STATION, AND--
#2

JANGLE
JANGLE
JANGLE

UH-OH! THE DRESS ME IN DISCO CLOTHING STORE IS UNDER ATTACK!

#2
SWIPE
1

#1
SMACK
DRESS ME IN DISCO

AND SO... TEAM PLANT!!!

NATE! QUIT LOOKING AT THAT WEIRD POSTER AND LET'S GET GOING!
COMING! GIVE ME A MOMENT!

AND SO...
DRESS ME IN
DISCO
50% OFF EVERY THING
DISCOUNT DOES NOT APPLY to ZOMBIES
NATE WILL BE HERE AS SOON AS HE CAN. MEANWHILE, LET'S TRY TO FIND OUT WHAT THE PROBLEM IS.

KA-BOOOOM!!!

SUPER BRAINZ IS PROBLEM, HERE!
SUPER BRAINZ IS ALWAYS PROBLEM!
WELL, AT LEAST WE AGREE ON SOMETHING.

AND SO...
C'MON, SCOOTER! WE HAVE TO CATCH UP WITH THE OTHERS!

AND, YOU KNOW, I REALLY LIKE HANGING OUT WITH YOU.
TOO BAD WE DIDN'T MEET IN TIME FOR YOU TO COME ALONG WITH BELCHER VON BOOM-THROAT AND ME WHEN WE WENT SEARCHING FOR DISCO CHOMPER!

DISCO CHOMPER IS A *LEGENDARY* PLANT. SOMEDAY, I'D *REALLY* LIKE TO SEE HIM. EVEN JUST A FLEETING GLIMPSE! BUT, NO LUCK!
MAYBE HE DOESN'T EVEN EXIST, BECAUSE I'M SURE I WOULD HAVE SEEN HIM IF HE WAS OUT THERE.
!!!

AFTER ALL, I'M *REALLY* OBSERVANT! *NOTHING* GETS PAST ME!
I'VE GOT A KEEN EYE! NOT EVEN THE SMALLEST DETAIL CAN ESCAPE!

OOPS! MY SHOELACE IS UNTIED!
SEE? A *LOT* OF PEOPLE WOULDN'T HAVE NOTICED THEIR UNTIED SHOE, BUT *I'M* ALWAYS ON THE ALERT!
BASICALLY, I'M IMMENSELY TALENTED.

GLOMPP!!!
OOPS. TIED MY SHOELACES AROUND MY THUMB.
AGAIN.

ANYWAY, SCOOTER. DON'T BE AFRAID OF THE ZOMBIES!
I'M WAY TOO OBSERVANT TO LET ANY OF THEM GET CLOSE!
GLOMPP!!!
AHHH!
AND...
MOUSETRAPS $3 FOR 5
GAHHH! MOUSETRAPS!
ALSO...
NELLIE'S NETS "OUR NET LOSS IS YOUR NET GAIN"
OOPS! FISHING NET!
GLOMPP!!!
WAHH! EGGBEATERS!
GBEATERS $5 (YOU KNOW WHAT THEY ARE FOR)
PLUS...

OKAY, WE MADE IT HERE SAFELY, SCOOTER!
GOOD THING I WAS KEEPING A CLOSE EYE ON THINGS!
UH-OH. DOESN'T LOOK LIKE THINGS ARE GOING WELL!
HEY!
NATE! FINALLY! TRY TO STOP THE ZOMBIES FROM GETTING INSIDE THE DRESS ME IN DISCO FASHION STORE!
US MAIL
I'LL TRY TO DEAL WITH SUPER BRAINZ AND...
...MR. STUBBINS!
OKAY, PLANTS! YOU HEARD HER! GET IN THE SHOPPING CART!
HURRY!
C'MON! LET'S TAKE THESE ZOMBIES DOWN! FIRE AT WILL ON...
SHOPPING CART TANK!!!
+1 speed!
+5 firepower!
THWOOM
THWOOM
P-TOO
P-TOO
P-BLAMM
P-BLAMM
THWANG
THWANG

"...THAT CONEHEAD ZOMBIE"!
"THAT FOOT SOLDIER ZOMBIE!"
"AND THAT 'CAMOUFLAGED' ZOMBIE PRETENDING TO BE A PLANT!"
SPAKK!
THAKK
WHAKK!
ZOOOM
WOOOSH!
BRAINS!

UH-OH! WE'RE TAKING FIRE AND THEY'RE CATCHING UP TO US!

NO PROBLEM!
GET TO IT, GUYS!

THOOM
WOOOSH!
THWANG
P-TOO
P-TOO
P-BLAMM
P-BLAMM
BOMBASTIC BLOVER TANK!!!
+5 speed! +8 firepower!

IS GOOD FIGHTING! BIG LAUGHTER! MANY SMILES!
PATRICE! I'VE CLEARED UP ALL THE ZOMBIES! YOU NEED ANY HELP?
SUPER BRAINZ HAVE SUPER FUN! HA HA HA HA!

NO NEED, NATE!
I BORROWED THIS LITTLE DEVICE FROM UNCLE DAVE!

"IT'S A REMOTE-CONTROL ACTIVATOR. MY UNCLE USES THEM TO CONTROL HIS UNDERARM DEODORANT.

"BUT I'M GOING TO PUT IT ON MR. STUBBINS' CAR!"
?!?!
WHAPP!!!

AND THEN ATTACH HIS CAR TO THIS MIRROR.

!!!
AND SEND IT AWAY DOWN THE STREET!
WHRRR
WHRRR
ZOOM

NO! MR. HANDSOME REFLECTION ZOMBIE IS...LEAVING?

DRESS
DISCO
COME BACK, MR. HANDSOME ZOMBIE!
WELL, THAT SETTLES *THAT*. THE STORE IS SAFE!
LOOPA BIDDLE QUABBLE!

KNOCK
KNOCK
KNOCK
UNCLE DAVE SAYS HE WANTS TO BUY A FEW DISCO SHIRTS AS LONG AS WE'RE HERE.

"ACCORDING TO MY UNCLE, THIS STORE HAS SOME VINTAGE CLOTHING...
"...INCLUDING THE VERY SHIRT WORN BY DISCO LEGEND *HILDA THE HIP* DURING HER LEGENDARY 1977 CHAMPIONSHIP SEASON. HE'S BEEN SAVING UP TO BUY IT."

BUT...!
OH, DEARIE ME. I'M SORRY. WE JUST SOLD OUR ENTIRE INVENTORY TO A NICE YOUNG MAN.
GUH?
SOMEBODY BOUGHT *EVERYTHING?* I WONDER WHO IT COULD BE?

MEANWHILE...
GLOMPP!!!
ROLL

SOON...
NOW THAT THE STORE'S SAFE, WE SHOULD GET BACK HOME.
I DON'T KNOW ABOUT THAT. MAYBE WE SHOULD TRY TO FIGHT BACK NOW, WHILE WE STILL HAVE A CHANCE?

"WITHOUT THE SOLAR POWER, NEIGHBORVILLE IS STARTING TO GO DARK. ALL THE LIGHTS ARE WINKING OUT.

"ALL THE TELEVISIONS WILL GO BLANK. THE BATTERIES IN THE ELECTRIC CARS WILL WASTE AWAY. UNCLE DAVE'S ELECTRIC NOSE HAIR TRIMMER WILL LOSE *ALL* POWER!"

YOU'RE RIGHT, PATRICE!
CRAZY DAVE NOT TRIMMING HIS NOSE HAIR IS *SERIOUS!*

IF YOU LIKE WORKING HARD
BUT DON'T LIKE GETTING PAID
COME AND WORK FOR ZOMBOSS
I'M THE FATE YOU CAN'T EVADE!
PLUS, WE *NEED* TO DO SOMETHING ABOUT THIS MUSIC.

WE HAVE TO DO THIS NOW, WHILE WE STILL HAVE A FIGHTING CHANCE!
IT'S TIME TO ASSEMBLE...
CITRON!

KERNEL CORN!

ROSE!

AND THE PIZZA DELIVERY GUY!
I GOT SOME PIZZAS WITH TRIPLE SUNSHINE, HERE. AND ONE TRIPLE LARGE WITH QUADRUPLE EVERYTHING.
OH, YEAH!

OKAY, EVERYONE! SNACK BREAK IS OVER! IT'S TIME FOR...
MUNCH
GOBBLE
MUNCH
MUNCH
GOBBLE

"...A NAP!"
ZZZ SNOZZ-GOBBLE-SNOZZZ ZZZ SNORE SNUFFLE
ZZZ ZZZZ ZZZZ SNUFFLE SNORE SNORK
BUT NOW, THE ATTACK BEGINS!
EVERYONE! KEEP AN EYE OUT FOR ZOMBOSS! CALL OUT IF YOU SEE HIM!
AND ALSO LOOK OUT FOR SUPER BRAINZ! HE'S THE REAL MUSCLE BEHIND THE ZOMBIE ARMY!!
AND WATCH OUT FOR MR. STUBBINS! HE'S THEIR HEART AND SOUL, AND AS TRICKY AS ZOMBOSS HIMSELF!
"C'MON, EVERYONE!"
LET'S FIGHT TOGETHER!

HURRY! MORE PLANTS OVER HERE!
POP!
GO!
POP!
POP!
UNFORTUNATELY...
EVEN KERNEL CORN CAN'T STOP THESE FOOT SOLDIER ZOMBIES ALONE!
POPPA! POPPA! CORN!
CITRON NEEDS HELP WITH THESE GARGANTUARS!
WOOOSH!
MORE PLANTS OVER HERE!
KRAKKK!
THOOOM!
WOOOSH!
ZOOOM!
ROSE! HURRY! THE PLANTS CAN'T STOP HIM!
SUPER BRAINZ TELL JOKE! KNOCK KNOCK! WHO THERE?
IT IS ME HITTING YOU WITH CAR! HA HA HA HA HA!
RUN RUN
AWESOME AUTOMATIC DONUT MACHINE
RETREAT! RETREAT!
WE'RE GOING TO HAVE TO RETREAT! WE CAN'T HOLD THEM!
WE'RE NOT Choco-late WE'RE Choco-ON TIME
HOP HOP RUN
SOOOT
THERE'S WAY TOO MANY ZOMBIES!
RUN RUN

AWESOME AUTOMATIC
DONUT MACHINE
WE'RE NOT Choco-laite WE'RE Choco-ON TIME
AN AUTOMATIC DONUT MACHINE?
NO TIME FOR THAT, NATE! THE SITUATION IS TERRIBLE!
WITH THOSE SOLAR PANELS COVERED BY THE MYSTERIOUSLY STRONG PAINT...THE ENTIRE CITY IS LOSING POWER!

"AND WITHOUT POWER, ALL THE CITIZENS WILL BE FORCED OUT OF THEIR HOMES..."
...RIGHT INTO THE MIDDLE OF ALL THESE ZOMBIES!
OKAY! YOU'RE RIGHT! WE HAVE TO FIND A WAY TO REGROUP AND--

?
TRIP
OOP!
BAFF
!

WHAT DID YOU TRIP OVER?
AH, DANG! IT'S SCOOTER'S WINDOW-WASHING AND WATERING-CAN-CLEANING SUPPLIES.
SORRY, SCOOTER! I SHOULD'VE BEEN--

LOOK OUT!
BRAAAINS!
THOOB!
THOOB!
THOOB!

P-BLAMM
SPAKK!
P-BLAMM

WOOOSH!
SP-TANG!
P-TINGG!

SPLOOOSH!

GLEAM!

WHOA.

HOW'D THAT HAPPEN? HOW'D SCOOTER MANAGE TO CLEAN UP THAT PERPLEXINGLY POWERFUL PAINT?
BREPPLE ZEPPLE FLOOM GOLLYBUM!
UNCLE DAVE SAYS THAT SCOOTER SEEMS TO HAVE MADE HIS CLEANING SUPPLIES...

"...OUT OF SOME OF MY UNCLE'S OLD DISCO-BALL-AND-EARLOBE-CLEANING CONCOCTIONS."
BELCH!
SPRAY
SPRAY

WHICH APPARENTLY HAS THE UNIQUE COMBINATION NECESSARY TO BREAK DOWN ZOMBOSS' SUPER-PAINT!
WIPE!

THIS...THIS IS IT!
THIS IS THE JANITORIAL WEAPON WE'VE ALL BEEN HOPING FOR!
CLAP CLAP CLAP CLAP CLAP

gurgle gargle
SPLURGG
SPLURGG
SPLOOSH
AND SOON...THE CLEANING BEGINS!
HELP ME TAPE THESE SPONGES TO THE SQUASH!
SWOOSH
SPLASH!
GREAT WORK, EVERYONE!
SCRUB SCRUB
GLOPPO SLOPPO FRAMM BIDDLE YOO!
AHH! GRRAWRR-BEAR, CALM DOWN!
WHAMM!
THWOPP!
SMAKK!
SPLUTTT
WE'RE MANAGING TO GET SOME OF THESE SOLAR PANELS CLEAN, BUT IT'S A LOT OF HARD WORK.
IF ZOMBOSS KEEPS PAINTING THEM, WE WON'T BE ABLE TO KEEP UP THE PACE.
WE *NEED* TO FIND OUT WHAT MAKES THIS PAINT SO POWERFUL!
UNCLE DAVE SAYS HE'LL DO SOME EXPERIMENTS ON THE PAINT AND CONSULT WITH SOME EXPERTS.
WE'LL *SOLVE* THIS!

BACK IN CRAZY DAVE'S LABORATORY!

TING
TING
TINNNG

SIZZLE

UNCLE DAVE! WHAT ARE YOU DOING?
WHAT KIND OF PAINT-RELATED EXPERIMENTS NEED SYRUP?

PANCAKE SANDWICH!
THAT'S BRILLIANT!

FILLBOOGER PABBSWOBBLE GRAK NOZZLE!
UNCLE DAVE SAYS HE'S CLOSE TO SOLVING THE PERPLEXING PAINT PROBLEM...
...BUT NEEDS TO TALK WITH SOME SPECIAL-ISTS.

Belcher von Boomthroat!
BELCH!

ICE CREAM CONE WITH A RAISIN FACE!

TOENAIL!

NUBSTUBBLE GLABBLE CROMSTOCK!
WHAT? EWW, REALLY?
HUH, WHAT'D HE SAY?

ACCORDING TO MY UNCLE DAVE AND HIS COALITION OF EXPERTS, THE REASON THAT THE PAINT IS SO POWERFUL IS BECAUSE OF...

"...SUPER BRAINZ'S DANDRUFF!
"APPARENTLY, EACH GALLON OF ZOMBOSS' POWERFUL PAINT HAS A FEW SPRINKLES OF SUPER BRAINZ'S DANDRUFF..."

THOKK
THOKK
HA! IS MUCH TICKLE!
"...HELPING TO BOND THE PAINT'S MOLECULAR STRUCTURE, MAKING IT NEARLY AS POWERFUL AS SUPER BRAINZ HIMSELF!"

THEN, IN ORDER TO STOP ZOMBOSS AND HIS EVIL PAINT, IN ORDER TO STOP THE ZOMBIES, IN ORDER TO SAVE EVERYONE IN NEIGHBORVILLE...
...YOU MEAN WE HAVE TO...?
YES.

WE HAVE TO CURE THAT DANDRUFF!

SOON...
YOU THINK CRAZY DAVE MIGHT HAVE ANY IDEAS?
I THINK WE'RE ON OUR OWN, HERE. HIS MIND IS KIND OF... SPORADIC?
AND AFTER WORKING ON THE SECRET OF THE ZOMBIE PAINT...
...NOW ALL HE WANTS TO DO IS WATCH HIS NEW FAVORITE TELEVISION SHOW.

The Chosen Bun

"IT'S ABOUT A HAMBURGER BUN WHOSE MARTIAL ARTS MENTOR IS KILLED...
"...AND WHO MUST STRIKE OUT ON HER OWN TO RECLAIM HER LEGACY.

"ALL UNCLE DAVE WANTS TO DO NOW IS WATCH THE SHOW. AND DRESS UP IN CHOSEN BUN COSPLAY.

"AND MAKE HIS OWN BRAND OF THE *BUN SAUCE* THAT NADINE, THE CHOSEN BUN, USES IN THE SHOW."

OKAY, EVERYONE! WE HAVE TO CURE THAT DANDRUFF ON OUR OWN!
ANYBODY HAVE ANY IDEAS?
MAYBE WE COULD JUST ENCASE HIS HEAD IN A BLOCK OF CEMENT?
I DON'T THINK THAT WOULD WORK.
SUPER BRAINZ'S HEAD IS BASICALLY ALREADY A BLOCK OF CEMENT.
HMM, AND HAVING THE BLOVERS BLOW HIS DANDRUFF AWAY WOULD JUST SPREAD IT AROUND.
SUPER GROSS!
COULD WE ENCASE HIS HEAD IN PIZZA?
W-WHY DO YOU THINK THAT WOULD WORK?
BECAUSE PIZZA CURES EVERYTHING!
NOT THIS TIME, AND... I'VE CHECKED ONLINE, AND REGRETTABLY NOBODY MAKES SHAMPOO FOR ZOMBIES.
OR DEODORANT, EITHER, UNFORTUNATELY.
WELL, WE HAVE TO THINK OF SOMETHING, OR ELSE ZOMBOSS WILL WIN!

ZOMBOSS HAS WON!!!
HA HA HA HA HA HA HA

TIME FOR STICKERS!

APPROVED BY ZOMBOSS
SMACK!

LET'S SEE...AH! HERE!
THIS BEAUTIFUL BUILDING!
SMACK!

THIS STATUE OF MR. STUBBINS!
SMACK!

SMACK!
THIS BUILDING FULL OF PEOPLE COWERING IN FEAR!

THESE IMPS GUARDING THE STREET!
SMACK!
EVERYTHING IS WORKING OUT PERFECTLY! HA HA HA!
ZOMBOSS APPROVES! HA HA HA HA HA HA!

YOU HEAR SOMETHING?
YEAH. SOUNDED LIKE...MANIACAL LAUGHTER?
OR MAYBE A FLOCK OF GEESE WITH GAS PAINS? ONE OF CRAZY DAVE'S ELECTRIC FARTING PIGS?

BUT...NO TIME TO INVESTIGATE! WE CAN'T LET THESE ZOMBIES STOP US FROM CLEANING THE SOLAR PANELS!
PEASHOOTERS! CHOOSE A LEADER!

!
POINT
POINT
POINT

SNIFF
SNIFF

AND SO...
SPLAP
P-TOO
P-TOO
THWAPP
THWAKK
P-BLAMM
P-BLAMM
SCOOT
SCOOT
ZOOOM
WOOOSH!

MEANWHILE...NOT FAR AWAY!
P-TOO
P-BLAMM
THWAP
G-DONKK!
I HEAR THE SOUNDS OF BATTLE!
HURRY, MR. STUBBINS! IT'S TIME TO CEMENT MY VICTORY!

OH, HOLD ON A MOMENT.
ERRRT!

WE HAVE TO WAIT FOR MY PERSONAL BAND.

"UNFORTUNATELY, THEY'RE NOT VERY FAST."
GRRR
TUG
TUG
PUTT!
PUTT!
PUTT!

"OR VERY GOOD."
HOWL
HOWL
HOWWWWL!

"OR VERY SMART."
Bark Bark
Pbbblapp!
PUTT!
PUTT!
PUTT!

MEANWHILE...
TRAPPED!

ONLY ONE THING TO DO, THEN.

YOU AND I. ONE ON ONE.

NOBODY ELSE TO INTERFERE.

NOBODY ELSE TO HELP US.

JUST THE TWO OF US, WITH NO MERCY ASKED FOR, AND NONE GIVEN.

"IT'S TIME TO SETTLE THIS THE OLD-FASHIONED WAY."

IT'S TIME TO SETTLE THIS IN THE WAY OF TRUE WARRIORS.

IT'S TIME TO...

...THUMB WRESTLE!

LET'S DO THIS!

C'MON, NATE! FIGHT FIGHT FIGHT!
BRAAAINSSS!

WHUMPFF!

OH, NO!
GRAH!

SWOOOP

HA! TOO SLIPPERY FOR YOU?
THAT'S BECAUSE MY THUMB IS COVERED IN PIZZA GREASE.

IT'S ALWAYS COVERED IN PIZZA GREASE.

BUT THEN...ZOMBOSS ARRIVES!
DRAT AND DANG! WE NEED TO WIN THIS BATTLE!
TIME TO ADD A LITTLE... EXTRA!
STINK BOMB RING!
OOOOG.
FLOP FLIP FLONGGO!
OH, NO! NATE'S REELING!
BABY BLOVER BLING
BLOOOOOW
HMMM.
GRRR!
HAMMER THUMB!
SWING!
TRAMPOLINE SHIELD!
SPROING!
Gumball Machine!
THAP
THOOT
THOOT
THOOT
THAP
THAP

Race car engine!
REVVV
REVVV
ROAAAARRR!

YUMM
TACOS!
YUMM
YUMMM!

C'MON, NATE! YOU CAN DO THIS!
CONFOUND YOU, PIN THAT THUMB!

MR. STUBBINS!
AHH! PRICKLY!

Belcher von Boomthroat!
BELCH!
SQUICK!

IMP IN A THUMB COSTUME!
RAIN
RAIN
RAIN
BRAAINSSS!
RAIN
RUN
RUN
RUN

Match called because of rain!
NEXT TIME! NEXT TIME!
CALM DOWN, NATE!

OON...
OKAY, EVERYONE! WE MANAGED TO STOP THE ZOMBIE ADVANCE ON *THAT* BLOCK...
...BUT THEY'RE STILL OVERRUNNING THE FEW REMAINING POCKETS OF RESISTANCE!
WE HAVE TO SLOW THEM DOWN TO GIVE US A CHANCE TO REGROUP!

SO I BUILT THIS MAZE!

THIS WAY, THE ZOMBIES WON'T BE ABLE TO FIND THEIR WAY THROUGH. THEY'RE ABSOLUTELY, FOR SURE, GOING TO GET LOST!
AND DO YOU KNOW *WHY?*
URGG. UGH.

BECAUSE THE ZOMBIES AREN'T VERY *SMART.* THEY'RE TOO *SIMPLE-MINDED* TO--
URFF. OOF.

NATE? WHAT ARE YOU DOING?
I'M TRYING TO GET THE *LID* OFF OF THIS *JAM JAR!*

UH. THE LID'S ALREADY OFF, NATE.
OH.

ANYWAY...LET ME GET BACK TO TALKING ABOUT HOW THE ZOMBIES AREN'T VERY SMART.

BUT THEN...
UH-OH. ACCORDING TO THESE PLANTS, THE ZOMBIES KEEP RE-PAINTING THOSE SOLAR PANELS!
IF WE'RE GOING TO SAVE THE CITY, WE NEED TO CURE SUPER BRAINZ'S DANDRUFF!

FLUTTER
FLUTTER
WE NEED TO--
HUH? WHAT ARE THESE?
FLUTTER
FLUTTER

ZOMBOSS
—Cordially invites—
all humans
to dinner
tomorrow night

DINNER? OH. THAT'S VERY NICE OF HIM!
NATE, I THINK HE MEANS ALL HUMANS WILL BE DINNER, TOMORROW NIGHT.
HE WANTS OUR BRAINS!

OH, DANG. I WAS HOPING HE'D HAVE MORE JAM.
I ONLY HAD ENOUGH FOR ABOUT HALF MY PIZZA.

BUT, NOW THAT I SEE WHAT HE'S UP TO ≥MUNCH MUNCH≤ I'M DONE FOOLING AROUND!
IT'S TIME ≥MUNCH MUNCH≤ TO GET AS MANY PLANTS TOGETHER AS WE CAN AND ≥MUNCH MUNCH≤ FIGHT BACK!
THIS IS NO TIME ≥MUNCH MUNCH≤ FOR EATING! THIS IS TIME FOR ≥MUNCH MUNCH≤ BATTLE!

MEANWHILE...
BLONKK WHONK THODDLE THUMM!

Stickers!

Clean!
SMACK!

SMACK!
Clean!

Clean!
SMACK!

SPAPP!
GREAT JOB

DUCK
SPAPP!

ICE CREAM
SPLURKK!

SMACK!
DAVE

AND ALSO...
HA HA HA HA HA HA HA HA HA HA HA HA
SMACK!

EVERYTHING IS GOING WONDERFULLY!
IT'S TOO LATE FOR THEM TO STOP ME!

"THAT INFERNAL ROSE IS BEING OVERWHELMED!

"KERNEL CORN WILL SOON BE POPCORN, AS WE TURN UP THE HEAT!

"CITRON IS BEING SQUEEZED!"

BRAINS!
BRAINS!
BRAINS!
AND AS MY ZOMBIES USE MY DANDRUFF-ENHANCED PAINT TO COVER UP MORE SOLAR PANELS, FASTER THAN THE PLANTS CAN POSSIBLY CLEAN THEM, THE HUMANS WILL BE FORCED OUT OF THEIR HOMES!
TOMORROW, AT LONG LAST, BRAINS!

EH? MR. STUBBINS? NEWS?

SQUICK!
YOU'VE FOUND THOSE IRRITATING CHILDREN? EXCELLENT!
THIS MEANS I'LL BE ABLE TO COMPLETE MY LIST OF THINGS TO DO!

1. Take over Neighborville
2. WASH my kitty Pajamas
3. Destroy Pesky CHILDREN

AND SO...FOOT SOLDIERS!

Scientist Zombies!

Captain Deadbeard!
ALL-STAR!
THWOONK!
THWOONK!
Gargantuar!

NATE! THIS IS BAD! WE CAN'T STOP ZOMBOSS AND ALL THESE ZOMBIES!
I KNOW! EVEN SCOOTER IS GETTING TIRED! BUT JUST KEEP FIGHTING, AND...DON'T WORRY.

I HAVE AN IDEA.

FIRST, A STURDY STICK!
GRAB!
BRICKS STICKS
I'M BRICK! YOU NEED A STICK?

Megaphone!
WRAP!
WRAP!

SNAP!
TRIGGER!

Stickers!

Frog!

AND NOW...

CLICK

BELLLLLCH!

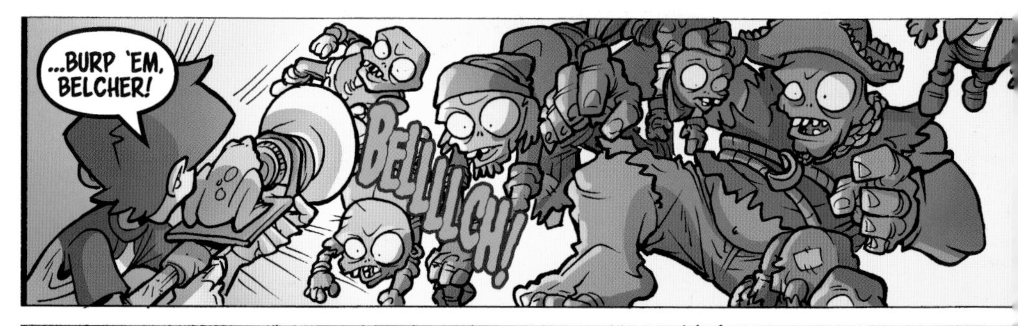
...BURP 'EM, BELCHER!
BELLLLCH!

BELLLLLCH!

BELLL
LLLCH!
SLURP SLURP
MUNCH
CURSES! TIME TO PLAY MY BIGGEST CARD!

HA! SUPER BRAINZ MAKES DRAMATIC ENTRANCE! TIME FOR MANY APPLAUSE!
FWOOSH!
QUABBLE?
BOOM!

PLORK!
OH, NO! UNCLE DAVE LOST THE ENTIRE JAR OF CHOSEN BUN SAUCE HE WAS MAKING!
GURGLE GURGLE
FLOB-TOBBLE!

GURGLE
GURGLE
YEAH. BUT, HEY... I THINK...

...IT CURED SUPER BRAINZ'S DANDRUFF?
WHAT? NOOO!

HMM. PLAY ALONG WITH ME, NATE.

OH, WOW, SUPER BRAINZ! YOUR HAIR IS SO LUSTROUS NOW! SO AMAZING! I HAVE, UM, ALL THE JEALOUSIES!!
YOUR HAIR LOOKS LIKE PIZZA! THAT'S A COMPLIMENT! YOU SHOULD QUIT FIGHTING AND GO LOOK IN EVERY SINGLE MIRROR!
SUPER BRAINZ IS BEING MORE HAND-SOME? IS POSSIBLE?

SUPER BRAINZ MUST GO SEE THE EXTRA HANDSOME-ING!
COME BACK HERE!
HA!

YOU...YOU CHEATED!
SPOOPLE!
MY UNCLE DAVE SAYS... TOO BAD!
YOU JUST LOST YOUR STRONGEST WEAPON!
AND, WITH THAT DANDRUFF CURED, WE'LL BE ABLE TO CLEAN ALL THE PAINT FROM THE SOLAR PANELS! IT'S TIME FOR NEIGHBORVILLE TO...POWER UP!

"AND NOW THAT WE CAN MOVE THE PLANTS AWAY FROM THEIR CLEANING DUTIES, YOU'RE IN FOR SOME REAL FIGHTING!

"BECAUSE WE'RE FIGHTING FOR THE PEOPLE OF NEIGHBORVILLE, AND WE WON'T EVER STOP!

"SO, SORRY IF THIS GETS YOUR GOAT, BUT IT'S TIME FOR A..."

...DECISIVE VICTORY!

AND SO, LATER...
OKAY, PLANTS; YOU HEARD UNCLE DAVE! IT'S TIME TO PRACTICE FIGHTING ZOMBIES!
EVEN THOUGH WE STOPPED ZOMBOSS THIS TIME, WE STILL HAVE TO FREE THE REST OF THE CITY.
THERE'S STILL A BATTLE TO BE WON!
GORBLE LAPP SWABBLE!

MEANWHILE...
C'MON, SCOOTER. THERE'S ONE THING WE DEFINITELY STILL NEED TO DO. A TERRIBLE PROBLEM THAT NEEDS TO BE SOLVED!
WE CAN'T POSSIBLY REST UNTIL IT'S DONE! OUR VERY SANITY IS AT STAKE!

YOU AND I NEED TO TAKE DOWN THAT ZOMBIE RADIO STATION.
AND THAT LAST SONG WAS, "EAT YOUR BRAINS!" BY ME, ZOMBOSS!
NEXT UP IS, "EAT YOUR BRAINS!" BY ME, ZOMBOSS, AND AFTER THAT, THE SAME SONG FIFTY MORE TIMES! STAY TUNED!

IT'S A LITTLE DANGEROUS BEING OUT HERE ALONE, BUT DON'T WORRY, SCOOTER.
YOU'RE WITH THE RENOWNED NATE TIMELY!

NO ZOMBIE CAN POSSIBLY SNEAK UP ON ME!

BECAUSE I'M WAY TOO OBSERVANT!
GLOMPP!!!

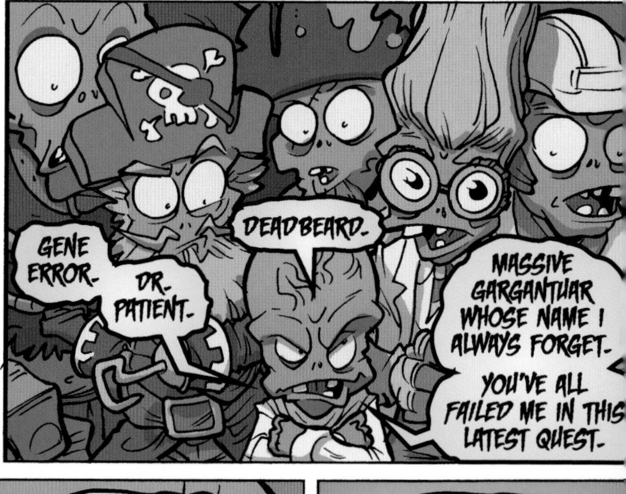

HA! HA! HA! HA! HA! HA!

THE END-ISH.

PLANTS VS. ZOMBIES: GARDEN WARFARE VOLUME 2

cover pencils by **TIM LATTIE**

PLANTS VS. ZOMBIES: GARDEN WARFARE VOLUME 2

cover inks by TIM LATTIE

PENCIL ART FROM *GARDEN WARFARE VOLUME 2* PAGES 38–41 BY ARTIST TIM LATTIE!

Book ______ Issue ______ Story Page # ______ Line Up Page # ______

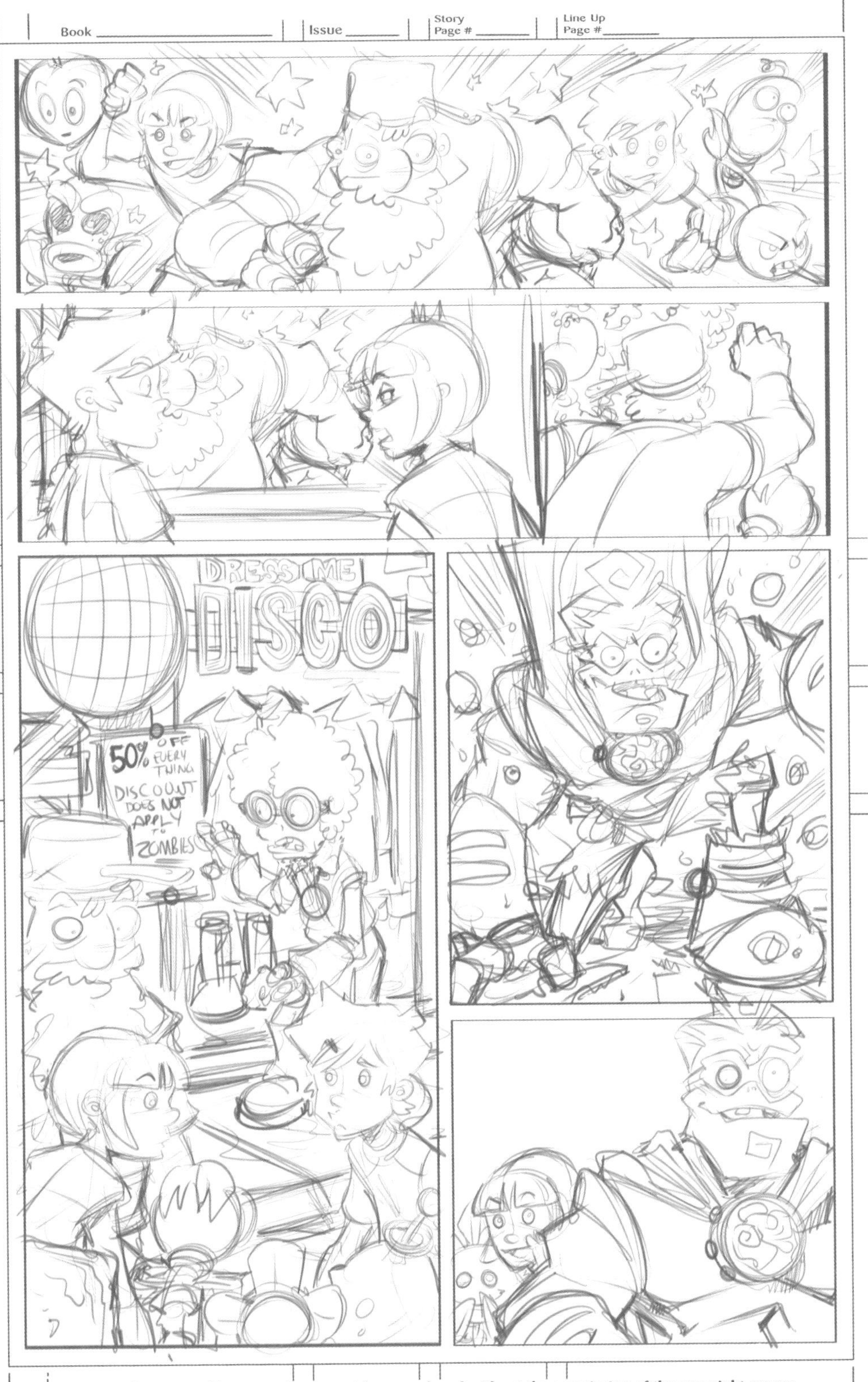

Book ______ Issue ______ Story Page # ______ Line Up Page # ______

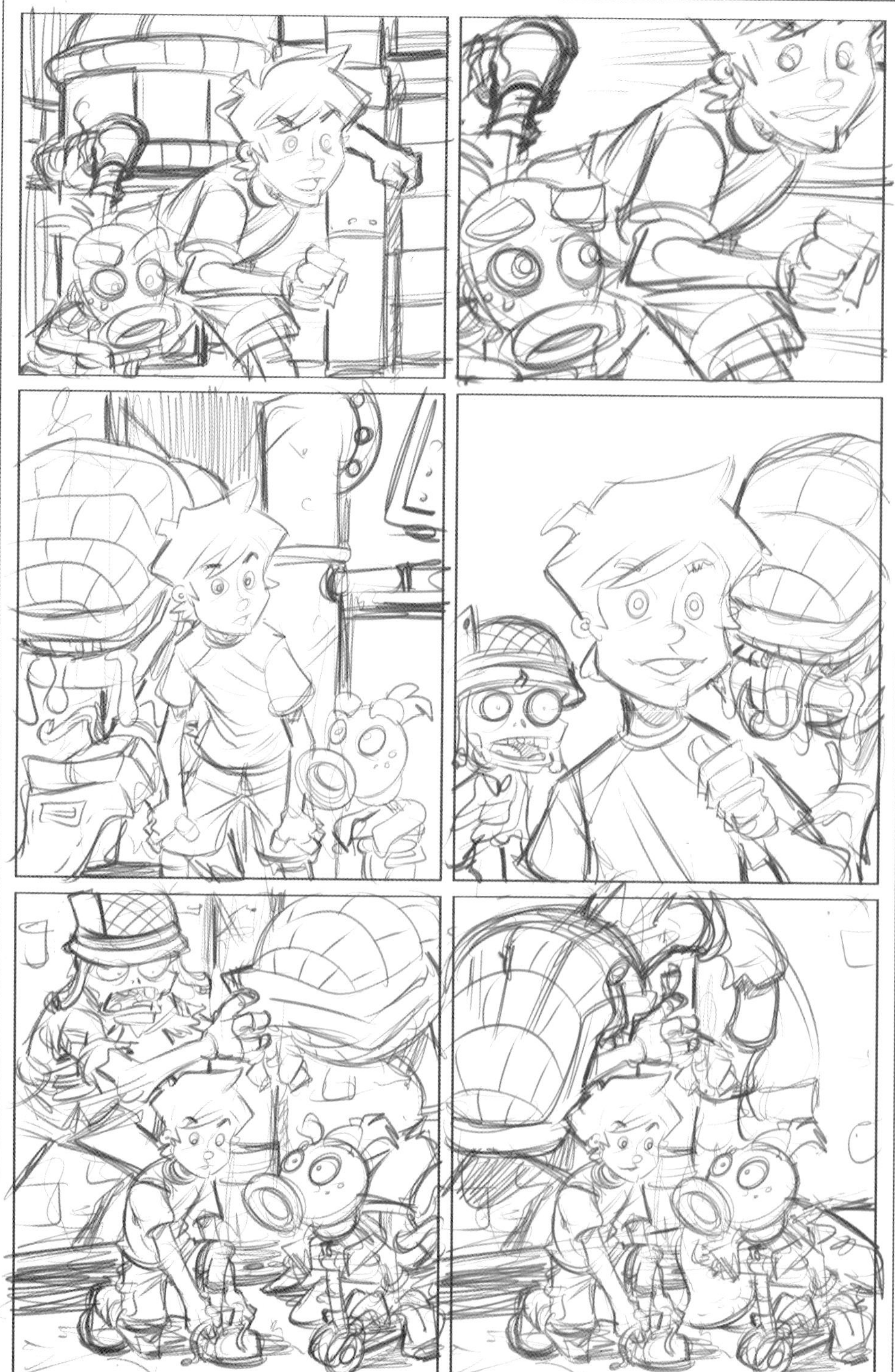

Book ________ Issue ________ Story Page # ________ Line Up Page # ________

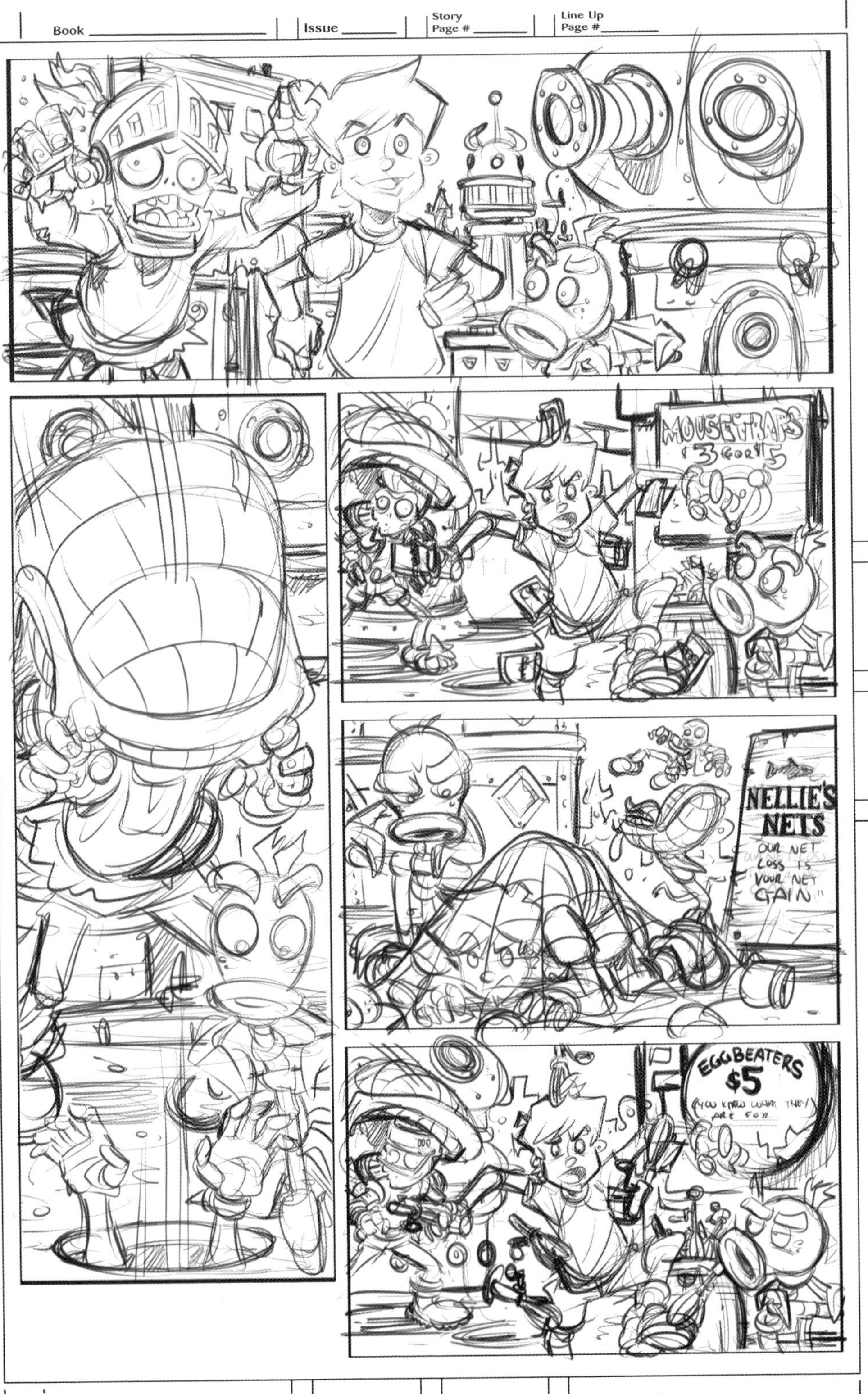

CREATOR BIOS

Paul Tobin

Tim Lattie

PAUL TOBIN enjoys that his author photo makes him look insane, and he once accidentally cut his ear with a potato chip. He doesn't know how it happened, either. Life is so full of mystery. If you ask him about the Potato Chip Incident, he'll just make up a story. That's what he does. He's written hundreds of stories for Marvel, DC, Dark Horse, and many others, including such creator-owned titles as *Colder* and *Bandette*, as well as *Prepare to Die!*—his debut novel. His *Genius Factor* series of novels about a fifth-grade genius and his war against the Red Death Tea Society debuted in March 2016 with *How to Capture an Invisible Cat*, from Bloomsbury Publishing, and continued in early 2017 with *How to Outsmart a Billion Robot Bees*. Paul has won some Very Important Awards for his writing but so far none for his karaoke skills.

TIM LATTIE, half artist, half amazing, was born and raised in Metairie, Louisiana. As a child he had a strong affinity for comic books and animation. This obsession led to him creating his own characters and stories. Later, he studied at NOCCA (New Orleans Center for Creative Arts) and SCAD (Savannah College of Art and Design). He now does graphic novels for IDW, Dark Horse, and UNICEF, as well as working on his creator-owned book about teenagers, time travel, and UFOs, called *Night Stars*! You can follow his work by going to www.LattieInk.com. Through the process of drawing this book, Tim has also discovered his true calling and has begun illustrating anti-plant propaganda for Zomboss's zombie army. Soon, not only Crazy Dave and his plants, but all of Neighborville shall kneel before ZOMBOSS!

Matt J. Rainwater

Steve Dutro

Residing in the cool, damp forests of Portland, Oregon, **MATT J. RAINWATER** is a freelance illustrator whose work has been featured in advertising, web design, and independent video games. On top of this, he also self-publishes several comic books, including *Trailer Park Warlock*, *Garage Raja*, and *The Feeling Is Multiplied*—all of which can be found at MattJRainwater.com. His favorite zombie-bashing strategy utilizes a line of Bonk Choys with a Wall-nut front guard and Threepeater covering fire.

STEVE DUTRO is an Eisner Award-nominated comic-book letterer from Redding, California, who can also drive a tractor. He graduated from the Kubert School and has been lettering comics since the days when foil-embossed covers were cool, working for Dark Horse (*The Fifth Beatle*, *I Am a Hero*, *Planet of the Apes*, *Star Wars*), Viz, Marvel, and DC. He has submitted a request to the Department of Homeland Security that in the event of a zombie apocalypse he be put in charge of all digital freeway signs so citizens can be alerted to avoid nearby brain-eatings and the like. He finds the *Plants vs. Zombies* game to be a real stress-fest, but highly recommends the *Plants vs. Zombies* table on *Pinball FX2* for game-room hipsters.

ALSO AVAILABLE FROM DARK HORSE!

THE HIT VIDEO GAME CONTINUES ITS COMIC BOOK INVASION!

PLANTS VS. ZOMBIES: LAWNMAGEDDON

Crazy Dave—the babbling-yet-brilliant inventor and top-notch neighborhood defender—helps young adventurer Nate fend off a zombie invasion that threatens to overrun the peaceful town of Neighborville in *Plants vs. Zombies: Lawnmageddon*! Their only hope is a brave army of chomping, squashing, and pea-shooting plants! A wacky adventure for zombie zappers young and old!

ISBN 978-1-61655-192-6 | $9.99

THE ART OF PLANTS VS. ZOMBIES

Part zombie memoir, part celebration of zombie triumphs, and part anti-plant screed, *The Art of Plants vs. Zombies* is a treasure trove of never-before-seen concept art, character sketches, and surprises from PopCap's popular Plants vs. Zombies games!

ISBN 978-1-61655-331-9 | $9.99

PLANTS VS. ZOMBIES: TIMEPOCALYPSE

Crazy Dave helps Patrice and Nate Timely fend off Zomboss' latest attack in *Plants vs. Zombies: Timepocalypse*! This new standalone tale will tickle your funny bones and thrill your brains through any timeline!

ISBN 978-1-61655-621-1 | $9.99

PLANTS VS. ZOMBIES: BULLY FOR YOU

Patrice and Nate are ready to investigate a strange college campus to keep the streets safe from zombies!

ISBN 978-1-61655-889-5 | $9.99

PLANTS VS. ZOMBIES: GARDEN WARFARE

Based on the hit video game, this comic tells the story leading up to the events in *Plants vs. Zombies: Garden Warfare 2*!

ISBN 978-1-61655-946-5 | $9.99

PLANTS VS. ZOMBIES: GROWN SWEET HOME

With newfound knowledge of humanity, Dr. Zomboss strikes at the heart of Neighborville . . . sparking a series of plant-versus-zombie brawls!

ISBN 978-1-61655-971-7 | $9.99

PLANTS VS. ZOMBIES: PETAL TO THE METAL

Crazy Dave takes on the tough *Don't Blink* video game—and challenges Dr. Zomboss to a race to determine the future of Neighborville!

ISBN 978-1-61655-999-1 | $9.99

PLANTS VS. ZOMBIES: BOOM BOOM MUSHROOM

The gang discover Zomboss' secret plan for swallowing the city of Neighborville whole! A rare mushroom must be found in order to save the humans aboveground!

ISBN 978-1-50670-037-3 | $9.99

PLANTS VS. ZOMBIES: BATTLE EXTRAVAGONZO

Zomboss is back, hoping to buy the same factory that Crazy Dave is eyeing! Will Crazy Dave and his intelligent plants beat Zomboss and his zombie army to the punch?

ISBN 978-1-50670-189-9 | $9.99

PLANTS VS. ZOMBIES: LAWN OF DOOM

With Zomboss filling everyone's yards with traps and special soldiers, will he and his zombie army turn Halloween into their scarier Lawn of Doom celebration?!

ISBN 978-1-50670-204-9 | $9.99

PLANTS VS. ZOMBIES: THE GREATEST SHOW UNEARTHED

Dr. Zomboss believes that all humans hold a secret desire to run away and join the circus, so he aims to use his "Big Z's Adequately Amazing Flytrap Circus" to lure Neighborville's citizens to their doom!

ISBN 978-1-50670-298-8 | $9.99

PLANTS VS. ZOMBIES: RUMBLE AT LAKE GUMBO

The battle for clean water begins! Nate, Patrice, and Crazy Dave spot trouble and grab all the Tangle Kelp and Party Crabs they can to quell another zombie attack!

ISBN 978-1-50670-497-5 | $9.99

PopCap

AVAILABLE AT YOUR LOCAL COMICS SHOP OR BOOKSTORE

To find a comics shop in your area, visit comicshoplocator.com.

For more information or to order direct visit **DarkHorse.com** or call 1-800-862-0052

PLANTS VS. ZOMBIES GRAPHIC NOVEL ZOMBOX

COLLECTING THREE DELICIOUS STANDALONE ADVENTURES AVAILABLE OCTOBER 2018!

Three *Plants vs. Zombies* graphic novels in one deluxe boxed set! The perfect addition to any PvZ fan's collection! This set also features an exclusive, double-sided poster and a brand-new piece of never-before-seen art by fan-favorite artist Ron Chan on the back of the slipcase! Spring an assortment of traps with Zomboss in *Lawn of Doom*, join the zombies and run away to the circus in *The Greatest Show Unearthed*, and finally, dive in and discover the mysteries underneath Neighborville's local aquatic retreat in *Rumble at Lake Gumbo*! This is a collection you won't want to miss!

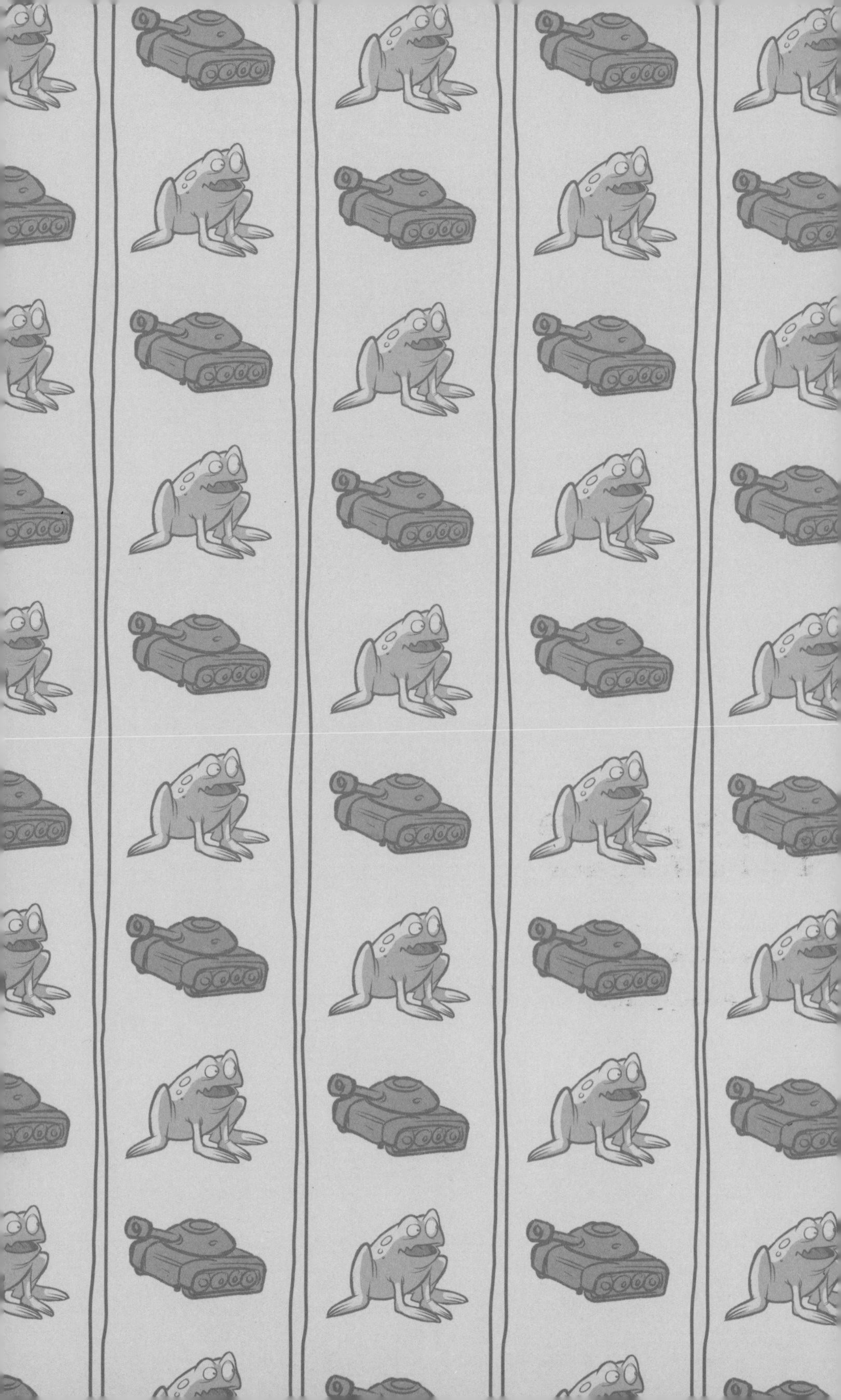